Little House

KATYA BALEN

Illustrated by
Richard Johnson

Barrington Stoke

Published by Barrington Stoke
An imprint of HarperCollins*Publishers*
Westerhill Road, Bishopbriggs, Glasgow, G64 2QT

www.barringtonstoke.co.uk

HarperCollins*Publishers*
Macken House, 39/40 Mayor Street Upper,
Dublin 1, DO1 C9W8, Ireland

First published in 2024

Text © 2024 Katya Balen
Illustrations © 2024 Richard Johnson
Cover design © 2024 HarperCollins*Publishers* Limited

ISBN 978-1-80090-255-8

10 9 8 7 6 5 4 3 2 1

A catalogue record for this book is available from the British Library

Printed and Bound in the UK using 100% Renewable Electricity
at Martins the Printers Ltd

This book contains FSC™ certified paper and other controlled
sources to ensure responsible forest management.

For more information visit: www.harpercollins.co.uk/green

"Beautiful and heartbreaking and glorious all at once. A little masterpiece" **STRUAN MURRAY**

"*Little House* tackles big world issues in a way that young readers will understand – a beautifully told story, light of touch, warm of heart" **JASBINDER BILAN**

"An enchantingly told, exquisitely illustrated story about a young girl's move from cosy innocence to a growing understanding of some of the sadnesses in the wider world" **NICOLA PENFOLD**

"Fierce, brave and compassionate" **NATASHA FARRANT**

"A beautiful, empathetic story about understanding the sacrifice sometimes needed to build a better world" **SARAH ANN JUCKES**

"Utterly gorgeous and beautifully written, this story about the interconnectedness of humanity and the importance of caring for others is both moving and full of hope" **JENNY PEARSON**

"Charming, tender and shines a sensitive spotlight on the true meaning of home" **A.M. HOWELL**

Also by Katya Balen:

Birdsong

Nightjar

For my German Girls – Laura, Insa, and now little Lotta. You make the world beautiful.

~ Chapter 1 ~

The night feels soft and warm when we arrive. The nightbirds are singing and the sound is gentle and low and all around us. Mum loops her arm round my waist but I wriggle away and let the shadows swallow me. The darkness is everywhere and it creeps and twists like the vines that snake up the side of the house.

The house looms ahead. Its shape shifts in the darkness and I shudder. It looks like one of those haunted mansions from the fairground. It's all edges and turrets and windows that flash with the whisper of ghosts and scattered stars.

I'd rather spend the summer hiding in the Yardley Fair Haunted House than have to spend it here. At least there'd be candyfloss at the fair. I could sneak out at night and play Hook-a-Duck and eat toffee apples until my teeth fizzed.

Mum rings the bell at the front door and it echoes in the still night air. An owl hoots and I twist to find it. You don't get owls in the city and it might be cool to see one just once.

But you do get funfairs in the city. And a summer filled with noise and music and cinema and friends and sleepovers and football in the parched dry park. I think of ice lollies that drip down your wrist and make your hot skin sticky with neon sugar. The summer everyone else is getting. Back home. But everyone else has nice normal parents who work in banks and schools and hospitals and shops.

The owl hoots again but I can't find it in the gloom. The stars are brighter here than at home but their glow only offers speckles of light on the gravelled drive. It's like the whole driveway is all the way at the bottom of the sea and the light is filtered and wobbling. The moon is a silvery O but it can't push back the night. There are no streetlamps or car headlights or glowing billboards and the dark has taken over.

Mum rings the bell again and keeps her long finger pressed down until a light flicks on somewhere inside. There's the crackle of a voice and the soft shuffle of feet.

I keep myself pressed into the shadows and I close my eyes. Just for a moment everything disappears and I imagine I'm back at home in my cosy bed with Fudge the rabbit. He's snuffling sleepily in his hay nest and a new summer's day is waiting for me when I open my eyes in the morning light.

"Juno, what on earth are you doing?" Mum hisses. Her cool hand is circled around my

wrist and my eyes snap open. I want to tell
her not to leave me and I want to tell her that
I don't want her to go. I want to tell her that
I am so worried and scared every single time
Dad goes away that it feels like my whole chest
will burst. Now Mum and Dad are both going
and it feels like my heart will splinter into a
thousand pieces.

"Mum," I whisper into the soft dark. "Please
don't go. Please stay back. Just stay with me
for the summer and we'll have the best time
ever, I promise. We can go to the funfair and
I'll make surprise pasta but not with mustard
this time. Please?"

"The mustard was definitely surprising,"
says Mum. There's a small smile on her face
but it slips away into sadness. "But you know
I can't stay, my love. You know I have to go.
It's not for long, Junebug. But I have to go. I've
not helped in so long. But I need to now. Those
tiny children. They've lost their homes. And

their mothers. Their fathers. They've lost everything and I want to give them something back. Something more than just words or a place to stay that's not their own. It's not enough to give people just enough. You have to give them hope. You have to give them a home. You have to make them feel like there is still beauty in the world. To make them feel that life can still be beautiful. They need that. I need to help give them that again."

I need you, I want to say. I want to shout it amongst the stars and let my voice bounce off the moon and startle the owls from the trees. I want my words to echo in the night air over and over until Mum listens. But me needing her isn't the same as the way the world far away needs her and so I can't say anything. It's not the same at all. But it still feels like my heart is trembling and I wish she would stay right here with me.

Then there's a rattle and the front door is open. My grandfather is standing in a doorway of amber light and Mum has already turned away.

~ Chapter 1 ~

Mum hauls my suitcase into the house and hugs her dad. The night is already pulling at Mum and she's fading.

Her hand is on the door handle before my suitcase has hit the floor. She kisses my forehead even though I hate that. She tells me to be good even though I hate that too. What else can I be but good all the way out here in the countryside? Unless I'm going to get into fox hunting or something, I can't really see a way to be bad. Just lonely.

But Mum looks me right in the eyes. She tells me that she loves me and that she'll be back so soon I won't even notice she's not here. Then she tells me to have fun and in a heartbeat she's gone.

I clench my fists and my nails carve tiny moons into the flesh of my hands. My eyes prickle but I won't cry. It wouldn't make a difference anyway.

Grandpa shuts the door with a click. I stand in the hall with the cold tiles pressing into my thin canvas shoes. He puts his hands into the pockets of his soft grey overalls and beams at me.

I haven't seen Grandpa in ages. Not since last summer. He's exactly like I remember. Tall but stooped. Overalls. His hands are rough and knotted from hours and hours in his workshop. His skin is stained darker by varnish and paint. Wood shavings dust his collar.

Grandpa asks if I'd like some tea or biscuits or cake and I shake my head.

"I've made a chocolate fudge cake," he says. He flaps his hands as he moves down the hall. "And some cinnamon biscuits. Or I could whip up something else. Whatever you fancy, pet."

I shake my head again.

"No, thank you," I reply.

"You must be tired," Grandpa says, and his eyes are kind. "And missing her."

I don't answer that bit. Instead I say in my most polite voice that I am very tired from the long drive and may I please go to bed.

I like Grandpa but I feel strange and out of place in his home. Normally he comes to us and I show him my fossil collection and we go and have pizza somewhere nearby. Then he gets in his very old and stuttering green car and disappears again.

But this time Mum is gone. Soon she'll be in the sky and she won't have time to call me and tell me anything at all. So I'll just have to imagine what she's doing. But every picture in my mind is terrifying and makes my heart bruise blue.

~ Chapter 3 ~

Grandpa lifts up my suitcase. It must weigh a ton because I've stuffed it with all my paints and sketchbooks. Then he leads me up creaking stairs that twist and turn in the belly of the house. My legs ache and I wonder how he manages it all because he's about a hundred years old.

Grandpa opens a faded yellow door and tells me to sleep for as long as I like and not to worry about a thing. He kisses my cheek and his skin is cool. I can see soft lines that spread like crumpled cotton but even so he looks like Mum. I say thank you and good night and I shut the door before he can say another word.

The room feels like something from a hundred years ago. It has a sloping yellow ceiling and the walls are dotted with sprigs of flowers that match the curtains. There's a carved wooden bed and a small chest of drawers and a three-legged stool in the corner. There's a jug filled with bright tulips and I stroke a pink petal that's as soft as rabbit fur.

Next to the jug are a pile of books with faded covers and a bear with one eye wearing a bow tie. It looks at me with its one glassy eye and I shudder. Creepy.

I turn the bear so its single eye is staring at the flowered wall and not at me.

I pick up one of the books. But I'm so tired and sad that the words swim and dance like twisting fish sparkling in a stream.

I don't bother to brush my teeth or wash my face or even put on my pyjamas. Instead I get under a patchwork quilt that's a thousand

stars all sewn together into a bright night sky.
I close my eyes but I don't fall asleep. How can
anyone sleep when their mum loves the whole
world more than them and when they've been
abandoned in the wild countryside? I'm used to

missing Dad. I'm not used to missing Mum. I'm not used to missing home.

Mum said it was too complicated for me to stay behind in Yardley Road and it would be nice to spend some time with my grandpa. She didn't ask me what I thought. Not once. And now Mum's gone to help someone else's children and I've got nothing left.

No Maya next door. No Fudge. No Yardley Road football tournament. No movie marathons and staying up until the sun starts to tip the sky into pink and yellow. No pizza parties or bowling trips. No flopping on DJ's trampoline and watching clouds change shape and wondering whether or not our teacher next year will be the kind who has a seating plan.

So I'm here and I'm all alone while everyone else gets their summer at home with their parents. Because their parents don't dart round the world when it starts to tear apart at its seams.

Their parents don't get phone calls about earthquakes and wars and floods and famines. All the things that have been churning and spitting and splitting countries apart since before countries were even invented. Their parents don't drop everything to try to glue the pieces back together. Their parents don't fly away and save somebody else's children and wipe the tears from their dusty faces. They don't tell them everything's going to be all right and try to make them feel at home again.

At least it just used to be Dad doing all that. I would stay home with Mum and try not to think about the bombs and the shaking earth and the diseases that could slip across the air like a warm breeze.

Mum stopped that work when she had me. She stayed home and the bad world was very far away. We were safe together in our warm little flat. We counted down the days until Dad came home and then we'd have a special party just the three of us because we were all back together and it was like a jigsaw puzzle. All our pieces fitting snugly together. A whole family.

But then Mum saw the TV reports and she heard Dad on the phone to the charity. He left again and she was very quiet for a few days. Then she told me she had to go too.

She had to go and save the world.

And now I feel like that jigsaw puzzle of our family is broken into a thousand pieces.

~ *Chapter 4* ~

The next morning the sun turns the room the colour of butter and the light slides off the walls. I blink and bury myself under the patchwork quilt but the smell of tea and bacon and eggs and toast curls its way under.

My tummy growls and I tell it to be quiet but it roars back. I get up and I put on shorts and a T-shirt. I can't find any socks in my suitcase, so my feet are bare and the tiles in the hall tingle like ice on my toes.

Grandpa is sitting reading a newspaper at the scrubbed wooden table in the kitchen. The back door is open and the heat of the day is already creeping inside. I can hear the hiss and screech of summer insects starting their morning songs. Grandpa gets up and says good morning. He pours me a glass of orange juice and goes to the stove.

"How would you like your eggs, Juno?" Grandpa asks. "Mavis is ready to provide." He waves a spatula over Mavis, a ceramic chicken, and lifts the top off. Underneath is a china basket filled with fat brown eggs.

"I don't know if your mother told you but I'm something of an expert. An eggspert." Grandpa grins at me and his face crinkles. I know I'm supposed to laugh but I can't.

I wonder if Mum's plane has landed. I wonder if she's walking down a dirt path past rows and rows of tents and whether the air is heavy with dust and the tang of sweat and blood and fear.

When Dad comes home, his stories about that world are always short and brutal. My imagination has to twist and turn until it finds the shape of the stories and I never know if the pictures in my head are true. They're always terrifying. But I always had Mum there to hold my hand and tell me everything would be all right. And now she's part of those stories and it makes my heartbeat start to race.

"'Juno, pet?" Grandpa asks. His voice pulls me from the stories – a whirl of screams and shouts and homes splintered into nothing but their bones. "Eggs? However you'd like them. Eggsactly as you command."

I arrange my face into a smile because that's what he wants. A muscle flutters in my cheek.

"Scrambled, please," I say, even though I don't care at all. My tummy wants food but my head doesn't mind what it is.

Grandpa nods and cracks eggs into a sizzling pan. He slices butter and twists salt and grinds pepper and whisks and whisks. He tells Mavis she's a very good girl for laying all the eggs.

I do my strange stiff smile back.

Grandpa sprinkles a tiny bit of something red and spicy on the top of my eggs. I sit down in front of a plate heaped with fluffy golden egg clouds and ruby strips of streaked bacon.

I fork the food into my mouth. At first it tastes like the dust and sweat and despair from the story in my head but I keep chewing and the flavours come alive. It is possibly the best breakfast I've ever eaten but I just say thank you and keep shovelling in mouthfuls of salt and spice.

"That's your mother's favourite, you know, pet," says Grandpa. He's pushing a piece of brown bread around his plate and mopping up the last of his buttery spiced eggs. "Your mum used to beg me to make it for her every Sunday. And every other day of the week too, actually. It always made her so happy." Grandpa gets a faraway look in his tired blue eyes and he's here and not here all in the same moment.

"Mmm," I grunt. I don't know what I'm supposed to say.

"I got a fair bit of grunting from her too, once she hit your age. You two are pretty similar, eh, pet?"

I stare at him. A scrap of egg falls off my fork.

"I don't think so," I say, and I stab the egg. My plate screeches under the metal of the fork and Grandpa winces.

I glare at the flower pattern that swirls across the tablecloth. I want to tell him that Mum and I aren't alike, not one little bit. I want to say I will never understand why Mum is the way she is and why she's decided to go away and leave me. That I don't understand why other people seem to be more important to her than I am. That I don't understand the fire that suddenly seemed to burn inside her when she saw that TV news report and how it glowed in her bones and spread and shone. I want to tell him that nothing I say or do ever makes her glow like that.

~ Chapter 5 ~

Time begins to sputter and stand still. The
plates have been stacked in the dishwasher
and I've wiped the table with the soapy cloth
Grandpa handed to me. Now there's nothing
to do.

Grandpa shows me dusty bookcases stuffed
with books that have titles like *Woodworking
for the Seasoned Amateur.* He points to the
wide wild garden outside and the old TV set
that flickers and strobes when I turn it on. And
that's it. That's everything there is to do here.

I think about getting my sketchbook
and trying to blur the world around me into

watercolours. But I just can't make myself want to do it.

Grandpa disappears off to the sprawling shed at the back of the garden and says I'm welcome to join him in his workshop. I peer inside and see benches dusted with wood shavings that curl and spill into the air.

There are planks and slices and splinters of wood in a thousand different shades and a whole wall covered in tools that look like they might belong in an operating theatre. There are half-open tins of varnish that leave gluey trails like metallic slugs and hundreds of paints in a rainbow of colours.

The air smells spicy and thick, like our flat at Christmas. There are carved boxes and half-finished chairs and tables scattered everywhere. It's a mess and it's very warm.

Grandpa picks up a saw and asks me if I'd like to make anything. But I've got nothing

I want to work on and I'm always rubbish at Design and Technology at school. Maya made a beautiful little windchime shaped like a nightingale last term. But when I tried to cut my piece of metal into the wings of a bird it twisted. I ended up with a slice of something that looked like it had been run over.

I decide to explore the house. It's huge. So many rooms and doors and stairs leading up and down and off to the side. Our flat in Yardley Road has four rooms and no stairs at all but I like that because it means Maya and I can roller-skate around easy-peasy.

I climb the stairs and hold tight to the banister. It's been carved so that delicate vines and leaves twist and grow along the wood. It looks like a forest stretching itself and climbing up towards the sky.

I go up another set of stairs. And then another. It feels like I'm rising up to meet the clouds. My lungs burn and my legs ache but I

keep going and the rest of the house starts to
fade away.

The stairs squeak like mice and they get
narrower and narrower. The grand staircase
below is forgotten and instead I am squeezed
tight between two walls. But suddenly the
stairs bloom and spit me out into the attic.

In my mind, attics are exactly where you'd
expect to find ghosts and murderers and
forgotten people and spiders. It's somehow

cool in here despite the heat of the summer day. The ceiling slopes this way and that, and it's like being in the belly of a ship.

There is a trickle of light, so I look up and see a skylight framing a bright blue square of sky. A few clouds puff and blow in the air and I watch them change from the smoky outline of a rangy cat to the gentle curves of a fisherman casting his line.

I love cloud-watching. The stories in them change second by second. The sky is the same everywhere but then also it's different in a blink. Maybe I could get a telescope up here and watch for shooting stars. Maybe I could make a wish.

Then something else catches my eye. It's a lump in the corner of the attic, draped in shadows and a sheet. If this was a horror film, then there would be someone, or something, hiding under it. Something with fangs or tentacles or inside-out skin. They'd leap out and gobble me up and that would be the end of me.

But this isn't a horror film. It's just a bright Thursday in July and I'm not going to be eaten by a monster. And I'm ten. I'm too old to be scared.

But as I walk towards it I can feel my skin prickling and my heart starting to flap. I lean in closer and pull the sheet. Suddenly a drip of something cold and wet catches me on the top of my head.

I shriek and leap back and land flat on my back on the dusty floor. The filthy sheet is draped over me like sagging grey skin. I can see a pipe, bent and dripping, snaking its way along the crooked ceiling. The drip wasn't monster venom or ghost ectoplasm. Just a plumbing problem.

I take a deep breath and crawl forward towards whatever the sheet was covering.

~ Chapter 6 ~

It's two cardboard boxes. Just boring old damp boxes that smell like mildew and are strung with spider webs. I roll my eyes. I wasn't expecting a treasure chest filled with rubies, or a haunted spellbook or anything, but I was hoping for more than this.

Still, there might be something cool inside. An old diary from a hundred years ago stuffed with secrets, or maybe a goblet that turns every drink into raspberry lemonade.

I peel the tape from the top of the closest box. It slides right off because its sticky glue dissolved years ago. The box flips open and the cardboard pretty much melts under my fingertips. The leaking pipe has dripped and dripped and soaked into everything.

I peer into the dark mouth of the box.

At first I think there's another box inside. A box in a box. I pull the damp cardboard sides of the outer box and they peel away like onion skin.

In the low light of the attic I can see the shape of the thing inside. The sharp lines. The grey stubble of stone walls brushed with painted ivy. The front door fading from red to pink. The sloped roof.

It's a little house.

It's cracked and faded and dusty and grey and old and neglected. I kneel up and lean forward and open the front. The house has been carefully divided into four rooms. It's raggedy and dusty and falling to bits, but it feels warm. It feels loved. It feels like a home.

Some of the four rooms in the house have fragments of furniture left inside but they've all been ruined by the water from above. Everything is damaged with water and age, and the wood of the roof has rotted away to almost nothing in one patch. It looks like a gentle breeze would blow the house to pieces.

There are no dolls inside but there are signs and scraps that this was once a home. I reach into a room on the ground floor and pick up a bathtub. It's greyed with age and grime but it has carved clawed feet like a lion's. They're red with rust now but the bath even has little taps and a plug hole.

I put the bathtub back and find a cupboard in the room next to it. Inside are real brown bottles labelled "BEER" and a clear glass one filled with something gummy and red that says "CORDIAL". There are tiny knives and forks

in a dresser. They're bent and twisted out of shape and their metal is dull but I can't stop looking at them. How can something be so small and so perfect?

On the second floor I find a brass bed with an actual blanket. It has worn away to threads and silk but I can just make out a gentle pattern of rosebuds.

I run my fingers all the way to the top floor, brushing against threadbare carpets and a broken wardrobe. Things that were once loved.

I try to pull the doll house towards me and away from the dripping pipe. It's wet and heavy and I can feel splinters spiking my skin. But as I drag it from the water, it creaks and groans. The wood beneath my fingers splits. I look down and see the front of the house is in my hands. The rest of the house is still underneath the pipe, ragged and gaping. I've broken it. I've broken this sad, beautiful little home.

I want to cry. I put the front of the house down and I blink and stare at the dust-motes dancing in the dark. They have diamond edges and they spin and land on the other damp box.

Something makes me lean forward and open it. The cardboard dissolves again and leaves wet pulp on my fingers but I wipe them on my jeans and stare down.

And there they are.

~ Chapter 7 ~

Inside the box are the dolls. Little dolls wrapped in plastic. Their faces peer up at me with eyes shining as bright as buttons.

I reach in and carefully lift one out. I peel back the layers of clear plastic wrapped around the doll's little body. It's about the size of my palm and so light that I can barely feel its featherweight in my hands.

The doll has a sweet round face with dark eyes and a rosebud mouth painted with a small swish of red. It is wearing faded blue trousers blushed with dust and a red-and-white striped top. Maybe it once had shoes but now its wooden feet are bare and someone has long ago painted the lines of toes.

A little shoeless boy. Something in my heart shifts and I'm not sure why.

I reach in again and unwrap another doll. This one is a bit smaller. She's wearing a dress decorated with yellow flowers and her mouth is curved into a smile. I stroke her hair and it is soft and silky between my fingers.

There are three more dolls. The next is clearly the father. He's taller than the others and he's wearing a checked shirt with real buttons. But some of the buttons are missing and his soft body is exposed. I tug the edges of his clothes together and he looks up at me. I blink down at his still, quiet face. He looks faraway and sad.

The final two dolls are wrapped together. The mother wears a dress that matches the little girl's, with those yellow flowers again. They're familiar but I can't quite place them.

A tiny baby doll is snuggled close to the mother's chest. He's just half the size of my little finger. He doesn't have any clothes.

Just a knitted blanket and a plain soft body that feels like it's weighted with rice. He shifts as I lift him and it's like picking up a sleeping kitten. I'm almost surprised not to feel the fragile beat of a heart in his tiny chest.

I examine his tiny wooden arms and legs and his sleeping face. He's all curled up in my palm like a bud waiting to unfurl. I stroke his blushed cheek with my finger.

A little family. All alone. Their house in ruins.

~ Chapter 8 ~

I get called down for lunch while I'm still holding the tiny family in my hands. Their arms and legs are tangled together and their sides are pressed close. I gather them closer and it's like their little bodies mould to each other.

I hear Grandpa's voice bouncing up the stairs again. The smell of onions and garlic frying in a pan is twisting into the attic.

I pick up the plastic wrapping and start to fold it around the dolls. I don't wrap them individually. They seem like they shouldn't be alone.

I'm about to put the dolls back in the box and push them from my mind because they're just dolls and I'm ten and too old for them. Also I'm hungry and I can hear Grandpa asking if I want chilli in my stir-fry.

But I can't do it.

I can't put the dolls back.

My hands freeze over the top of the gaping mouth of the box. The plastic wrapping rustles between my fingers. I look down and I see five small faces gazing up at me and my heart squeezes.

They are so lost and alone and the box is cold and damp and always as dark as night.

I gather the family to my chest. On my way downstairs I tuck them under my pillow while I decide what to do. I slip the mother gently next to her children and I see a repeat of her dress. The curtains in my room. They have the same little yellow sprigs of flowers. I look at the tiny careful stitches that tuck and nip and wrap the dress around the mother's body. I wonder who cared enough to do that.

~ Chapter 9 ~

Downstairs I eat mouthfuls of monster spicy stir-fry. My eyes are streaming and my nose is running and there's a film of sweat on my lip, but all I'm thinking about is that little dress and those little dolls.

"Have you thought about what you might like to do this afternoon, pet?" asks Grandpa as he adds extra hot sauce to his bowl. He's a chilli-eating machine. He isn't even sweating.

I wipe my forehead and look out towards the flowers shivering in the breeze.

"Can I come to see your workshop?" I ask. I twist noodles round my fork and don't meet his eye.

"Of course, pet," Grandpa replies. "That would be marvellous. You can help me build a rocking chair if you like. My issue at the moment is that it's not rocking. Tricky business. Or you can choose your very own project. It's nice to have a project. Keep the hands busy and the mind calms itself. Your mum and I used to make lots of things together. That was a lovely time."

We walk out across the garden and into the workshop. Grandpa points to the carved rocking chair he's working on and says something about needing to rethink the runners. I'm not listening. I'm looking at the planks of wood and wondering.

"How would I make a box?" I ask. "A box with ... other boxes inside it. Like, divided up."

Grandpa looks confused. He takes a pencil from behind his ear and grabs a sheet of dusty paper from one of the workbenches.

"Draw it, pet," Grandpa says. "It's always best to work from a bit of a plan."

He gestures to the walls and I see sheets of yellowed paper tacked around. Some of them have detailed drawings with lines that flow and cross and twist to show the angles and beauty of a carved bird. Some of them just show scribbles that make no sense at all to me.

I take the pencil and I start to draw. I let my mind and my hand fizz together. I stop thinking properly and I just let the picture fall onto the page. My fingers start to ache and I keep going. I only stop when the side of my palm is shining silver with pencil smudges and the page is filled.

It's the little house but I've put it all back together with my pencil. Four rooms and a triangle for a roof. Grandpa looks at the paper and he raises his bristly eyebrows ever so slightly. But he nods and tells me that I'm very good at art.

"How come you want to make this then, pet?" he asks.

Grandpa is still looking at the paper and I blush bright red. I don't want to tell him about the sad little doll family. It feels babyish and silly and somehow the most important thing in the world.

I don't think I can fix the old house. It's bloated and rotten and there's water all through its bones. But I can build a new house. I can give the family a home again. I can make something beautiful.

"Dunno," I say. "Just do. Not sure. Can we?"

"It should be easy enough, pet," Grandpa says. "The best thing to do is make a box and divide it after. Come and choose your wood, and I'll show you how."

I wander over to the stacks of wood and run my hands over the knotted smoothness. There's every colour here. Wood streaked with honey and wood as dark as a blackbird's wing and wood as pale as paper. I choose some wood that is streaked and marked with a grain that looks like clouds swirling in a golden sky. Grandpa nods his approval.

For the whole afternoon Grandpa shows me how to measure and cut, saw and sand. My hands become rough and blistered but I don't even notice. I make mistakes and there's sawdust in my hair and my ears and eyes and

probably in my lungs too. But I don't care because the shape of something is emerging.

There are slices and squares of wood. We piece them together with glue and joins and tiny nails the size of my fingernails. The sound of hammering and the screech of sawing starts to grow its own rhythm. It becomes like the beat of my heart and the breath in my lungs.

Grandpa stops to make us hot tea and warms up scones with jam and clotted cream. I don't want to stop, so I keep sanding just like he shows me but my mouth is as dry as the sawdusted air. I take a sip of the steaming tea and it scalds and soothes me all at once.

"It looks beautiful, pet," says Grandpa as he stands back to look at the shape we've made.

I stand back too and I look at it for the first time and he's right. It's incredible. It's a real little house. An upright rectangle with four rooms inside, divided by wooden walls. The roof is angled in a perfect triangle and inside it is another room. Just like the attic where I found the dolls.

The little house doesn't have a front yet but I like that. It's open and airy and I can see every join and cut and line we've made. I run my fingers along the smooth floors and the straight walls. A few hours ago this was just a pile of wood and now it's something else completely. It's a home. That's a bit like magic.

We stop because the light has faded and Grandpa's eyes aren't what they used to be. He says artificial light is too harsh and stops him understanding the wood. I don't really understand him or the wood but we go inside anyway. He cooks something that's warm and spicy and smoky and full of chickpeas. I help roll out flatbreads and cook them until they're puffy and lined with charcoal.

That night I lie the dolls next to me on my pillow. I tell them it'll be ready soon and that everything is going to be all right and their faces look bright with hope in the silver moonlight.

~ Chapter 10 ~

"Just need to give her a front and a lick of varnish and she's all done," says Grandpa. He is drinking a huge coffee because the sun is only just lifting into the sky. I was up early because I was so excited to finish. Grandpa says he always gets up early anyway.

He reaches for another slice of wood and we talk about doors and windows and hinges. I nod and try to slip some of the new words and knowledge inside me so I can keep it for ever and always know.

We make the front. We measure and then cut the wood so it matches the rectangle plus triangle shape of the house. Grandpa somehow carves a perfect little wooden door and puts it on tiny hinges. Each window is a cluster of four small squares in each corner of the front piece. Grandpa cuts those too because they're tricky and fiddly but he shows me how and I try the final window set myself. They don't look as neat as his but he says they do and I puff with pride a little bit.

I paint the sides of the roof in a grey-blue colour. Meanwhile Grandpa fiddles with hinges and sands the cuts we made for the windows and doors. My skin is covered in paint and starts to look a bit like I'm part Smurf but the roof looks brilliant. I love painting. You can make something beautiful.

Grandpa and I attach the front so it swings open on hinges. He tells me to paint the front door whatever colour I like. I think about his house and the buttercup door that looks so bright and cheerful and I choose yellow. Grandpa beams.

"Your mum chose that colour for our front door," he says. "I've always loved it. She used to say it was like stepping into sunshine."

"Hmm," I say. I am painting the door carefully with a little paintbrush. My hand slips and stains the tips of my fingers yellow and now my skin looks like modern art.

Grandpa sighs and cracks open a tin of varnish and starts to brush the wooden sides of the house. We paint together in a gentle silence and the house gleams new and bright.

It's nearly ready.

~ Chapter 11 ~

I sleep with the dolls curled next to me on my pillow again. It feels a bit bonkers but it also feels right. I whisper to them that they'll have a home soon.

"I promise," I say. "I promise."

In the morning the summer day burns gold and blue all over again. I am too excited to eat eggs and toast. Grandpa seems to understand because he lets me go straight to the workshop to see the little house.

It stands proud in the morning light. I touch it and the paint is as dry as a bone. The yellow door is ajar.

It's ready.

Grandpa and I carry the little house inside together and up the stairs to my room. I shift the books and the creepy teddy off the chest of drawers and Grandpa puts the house down. We stand back to admire it. Part of me wants to show him who it's for and why I've done it. But another part of me stays folded tight shut and I don't want to share.

Grandpa doesn't ask and he doesn't stay. He just ruffles my hair and turns to go.

"Beautiful work, Juno," he says as he disappears out of the door. "Perfect, beautiful work."

I grab the dolls from under my pillow and I swing open the door of the house and put them inside. I arrange them in one room. Mum on the floor with the baby on her lap. Dad sitting next to her. The children close together facing their parents, their hands tangled and heads resting on each other.

"There you go," I say. "All better."

But it's not.

It's not all better.

It's better.

But not all.

It's not right.

Not yet.

I stare at the little family all curled up together in their new house. Their new empty house. Bare wooden floors and walls. Nothing else at all. It's better than a dark cardboard box and a damp attic and plastic wrapping and being kept apart. But there's so much more, I think. There's so much more than that.

Mum's voice floats towards me and it sounds so close and real that I jump. But it's just her words whispering inside my head.

"It's not enough to give people just enough. You have to give them hope. You have to give

them a home. You have to make them feel
like there is still beauty in the world. To make
them feel that life can still be beautiful."

Each word feels like a little electric shock
zipping across my brain. I wasn't really
listening when Mum talked about her trip and
about the faraway world and the loss and the
death and the homes torn apart and broken
to pieces. All I could think about was Mum
leaving our home. Leaving me.

But her words are singing now.

I want to make this house beautiful. I want
to make it a home.

～ Chapter 12 ～

The problem is, I don't know how to make the house beautiful and a home. I don't know how to take a tiny blank space and fill it with tiny beautiful things. It's not something I've ever thought about before.

I think about my bedroom back in the Yardley Road flat and what makes it warm and bright and cosy and homely. It's a thousand things and a million memories all woven into the quilt and the pictures on the walls and the big soft rug that Mum brought home from somewhere far away. It's the books I've read over and over and the games I'm too big for now but that sometimes Maya and I play anyway.

It's everything.

How can you go and make all that from nothing?

But I have to try.

The wooden rooms feel sharp and hard and stark. I think that blankets and cushions and rugs and paintings might soften their edges a bit. But I don't really know how to make those things. I mean, I can do a loopy stitch because Mum showed me once. Her stitches were small and careful and neat, and mine were a tangle of thread and crossness, but I know the action at least.

I rush downstairs and get the wooden sewing box down from the bookshelves. It's dusty and no one can have used it in forever. The rusted hinges squeak when I open it.

Inside is a treasure chest of threads in every colour, arranged in neat rows. There's a section filled with scraps of fabric and another stuffed with sharp silver needles.

I take the whole box upstairs and I cut squares of green silk and red cotton and yellow velvet. I hem the edges to stop them fraying. They look a bit misshapen and odd but they're soft blankets and rugs. I cover the floors with them and the house looks warmer and brighter already.

I find a square of the yellow-flower fabric that matches the curtains and the dresses. I spend extra time making it into a blanket that's as perfect as possible, then I wrap up my little people in it so they're toasty and cosy and warm and together. I wonder which hands cut this square out and which hands stitched those dresses together.

Grandpa calls me for lunch. I shovel spinach and potato curry into my mouth as fast as I can without choking myself or looking rude. I actually do both because a bit of potato gets stuck and I cough it out across the table. But Grandpa just rolls his eyes and hands me a napkin and says he'll clear the table if I'd like to go and read or something. He says the word "something" strangely. It sounds all heavy and knowing. I know I could ask him for help. But I don't want to. I want to do this myself.

~ *Chapter 13* ~

I get out my paints and my sketchbook. I cut out pieces of thick watercolour paper and I paint tiny pictures. I paint the sunflowers outside and I paint the owl I didn't get to see and I paint the little family all together. I paint a wiry grey dog and I paint a ship sailing far away. I have a go at modern art with splotches and swipes and stripes.

I use dabs of glue from a gluestick in my pencil case and stick the pictures to the walls of every room. The house glows. The dolls somehow look more relaxed. Like they're moulding themselves to the shape of the house, leaning into it, becoming part of it.

But they don't have any furniture. I chew my lip. The dolls should have furniture. I think about the house upstairs in the attic. The scraps left inside it.

I scamper up the stairs and back into the dust-mote darkness. The damp smell makes me sneeze but I wipe my nose on my sleeve. Mum hates it when I do that.

I grab the furniture but it's too much for just my hands so I turn up the bottom of my

T-shirt to make a kind of pouch. I fill it and then I walk down the stairs extra carefully.

Back in my bedroom I sit on my bed and empty my T-shirt onto the bedcovers. I grab the furniture out greedily. A double bed. Two singles. A cot. No mattresses. A table and four chairs. A wooden sofa with no cushions. Kitchen cupboards. A wardrobe. An iron bath with tiny taps. Even a tiny loo with a handle for the flush.

But it's all in bad condition. The furniture looks worse in the sunlight than it did in the attic, and it didn't exactly look great in there. The wood is damaged and dull. The bath is rusting. I open the kitchen cupboards and the pile of miniature jars and bottles fall out. Their labels are peeled and faded.

I know what I have to do. I gather up the things back into my T-shirt pouch. I carry them carefully down the stairs and out into the garden and into the workshop.

~ *Chapter 14* ~

Grandpa is already in the workshop.

I unpack the furniture onto the workbench. I place each piece side by side. Grandpa picks up a bed and starts to sand it, handing me a piece of fine sandpaper too. I pick up another bed and copy his movements. Gentle, careful. We rub away the old and the rotten. We make the beds beautiful.

We work in silence for a while. The only sounds are just the scrape and scratch of sandpaper on wood.

Then my voice breaks the rhythm.

"Where did these come from?" I ask.

"The attic, pet," Grandpa replies. "I should think that's where you found them. Unless that scampering I've been hearing up there is a giant squirrel infestation."

"I know they came from the attic," I say. "But before. Before the attic."

I know the answer before Grandpa says it.

"That would be your mother, pet. She and I made these, so many years ago. We made that house too. Together."

"Why?" I say.

"Ah, pet. It was a sad old time," Grandpa says. "Your grandma, your mum's mum, she'd just died. Your mum was only your age. She didn't know which way was up. Everything was terrible. She didn't love the world. So she and I started small. We worked together, in

71

here. Sometimes we talked. Sometimes we didn't. We built a little house and we filled it with beautiful things. And a little family. Your mum loved it. She made it perfect."

"Oh." It's all I can say. There's so much sadness and beauty and hope and loss swirling around us that I can't breathe as deep as I need to.

"Aye," Grandpa says. "Your mum wanted to make everything perfect. She wanted to make everything good. That's why she did the work she did. She wanted to help others find hope and beauty when there wasn't any. And that work meant she got to meet your dad, and then she had you. And your mum loved you like nothing on this earth. I've never seen a love so fierce and bright. She told me, *'I want to give Juno the world. I want to give my daughter the whole world.'* And she stayed with you and she gave you your little world. But now the world she wants to give you is bigger than that. And

I think that's why your mum is out there. She's trying to make the world perfect. For you."

I blink. I swallow. My eyes are hot and there's a rock in my throat.

"But I just want Mum here," I say. My voice wobbles and cracks and falls straight to the floor. I think about what makes a home and I think about the mess and the disasters and the worry of the world. I think about how it's all so much better when Mum is with me and it's us and we're together. "I just want her here," I say again.

"I know, pet," says Grandpa as he sands the side of the rusty bath. "I know that. But I wanted you to understand. To try to understand."

~ Chapter 15 ~

I put the mended furniture in my little house.
I tuck the children up in bed and I sew cushions
for the sofa and let the mum and dad stay up
late. Everyone looks calm and happy and at
home. Perfect.

The next few weeks pass in a blur of
sunshine and sewing and learning to cook.
Grandpa teaches me how to make Japanese
ramen and American pancakes and spaghetti
carbonara. We travel round the world every
mealtime.

In the evenings I stitch tiny cushions and
blankets and I make the little boy a pair of

shoes from cork and scraps of old leather.
Grandpa reads books about different kinds of
woodworking joints or something. It's kind
of lovely.

On a bright Saturday morning Mum comes
back. I hear the crunch of a car on the gravel
outside and I run down the stairs and throw
open the buttercup door.

Mum is creased from being folded up on
planes and buses and cars. She has smudgy
shadows under her eyes and she's thinner, but
she's here. She's here. She's back.

I press myself flat against her and it's like
I'm trying to stitch myself to her. Mum pulls
me even closer and she smells my hair and
tells me she loves me.

There are cups of tea and Mum has a very
long hot shower, then Grandpa disappears
to do something with a dovetail joint in his
workshop. I take Mum's hand and I lead her

upstairs shyly. My heart is thumping in my ribs.

I show her my little house. I show her what I've made.

Mum gasps.

"Oh, Juno," she says. "Oh, Juno. It's so perfect. It's so beautiful. It's so *you*. And my goodness. It's so like the house I built. So very much like it. Goodness. I haven't thought about that little house in years. I loved it so much. I put everything into it. It was everything, for a while. It was a whole world, right here in one room." Mum traces the roses and ivy that twist around the tiny buttercup door.

"I remembered what you said," I say, and I'm looking at my toes instead of at her. "About things needing to be more. That just *enough* isn't good enough. I understand a bit now. I understand why you went. Why you had to go."

Mum runs her hands through her hair.

"I know you were angry with me, Juno," she says. "And I understand. I do. But I had to go back to help. I stayed away for so long and I watched your dad go off and I kept you and me safe and cosy in our little world. I'd try to forget about everything else happening out there. But I couldn't. And it's not good enough to be horrified about the horrors of the world and then to switch off the TV and go to bed safe and sound, it all forgotten by the morning. That's not good enough for me. It's not fair. It's not how things get better. It's not how the world gets fixed. The biggest thing I can ever give you is the understanding of how important it is to care and to do something to show you care."

I curl myself round Mum and I lean my head on her shoulder. I think about how much I cared about the dolls and their home. How that felt. How I couldn't stop until things were better.

"I don't want you to stop helping," I say, and I mean it. "I don't want Dad to stop either. I don't want that at all. I want to help too, when I can."

And Mum nods and her eyes are soft and bright with tears and she puts her arms around me. For a little while we just stand together and look at the little house that is full of care.